D1512555

LET'S BOWL!

by Amy Keating Rogers
Based on "Foster's Home for Imaginary Friends"
as created by Craig McCracken

SCHOLASTIC INC.
New York   Toronto   London   Auckland   Sydney
Mexico City   New Delhi   Hong Kong   Buenos Aires

No part of this publication may be reproduced, or stored in a
retrieval system, or transmitted in any form or by any means,
electronic, mechanical, photocopying, recording, or otherwise,
without written permission of the publisher. For information
regarding permission, write to Scholastic Inc., Attention:
Permissions Department, 557 Broadway, New York, NY 10012.

ISBN 0-439-87471-8

TM & © 2006 by Cartoon Network.
CARTOON NETWORK, the logo, FOSTER'S HOME FOR IMAGINARY FRIENDS,
and all related characters and elements are trademarks of and ©
Cartoon Network.
(s06)
Published by Scholastic Inc. All rights reserved.
SCHOLASTIC and associated logos are trademarks
and/or registered trademarks of Scholastic Inc.

Designed by Kim Brown

12 11 10 9 8 7 6 5 4 3 2 1   6 7 8 9 10/0

Printed in the U.S.A.
First printing, September 2006

MADAME FOSTER'S FURY

SLAM! The door to Foster's Home for Imaginary Friends flew open with a bang. The home's founder, Madame Foster, stormed in. She was carrying her bowling bag. Most days, tiny, gray-haired Madame Foster was very cute, quirky, and adorable. But not today. Today she was very angry.

"Simply unbelievable!" she ranted. "The stealing and the taking and the bribing!"

As Madame Foster shuffled in, she passed Wilt, a tall, red Imaginary Friend who lived at the house. Wilt's one good eye was wide open. His jaw was dropped in surprise. He had

never seen Madame Foster so furious.

"Why, I should have, and I would have if I could have, but no way, nohow!" continued Madame Foster. She stomped by another Imaginary Friend, Eduardo. Although Eduardo looked like a big, scary monster with pointy teeth and horns, he was really a sweetheart. Hearing Madame Foster talk this way actually made him scared.

"Downright nasty, I say! Having the pluck to pluck up my chickens!" cried Madame Foster as she passed Coco, the bird/airplane/palm tree Imaginary Friend. Coco looked just as confused as her friends were at Madame Foster's strange behavior.

"I should have git up and gone while the iron was hot! But did I heed my own warning? Nope!" said Madame Foster as she reached

the stairs. Standing there was Mac, a young boy, and his Imaginary Friend, Blooregard Q. Kazoo, known to almost everyone as Bloo. Mac was just as stunned as Wilt, Coco, and Eduardo at Madame Foster's tirade.

But Bloo was paying no attention. As usual, he was more interested in himself. Today he had his hands caught in a Chinese finger puzzle. He kept pulling his blobby blue hands away from each other, which only made the finger puzzle tighter.

"Snatching up my teammates before the final bell. Right before the last game! The gall!

The gumption! The nerve! That lousy, no-good Jerkins!"

BANG! Madame Foster dropped her bowling ball on the ground with a thud. Mac, Wilt, Coco, and Eduardo all jumped at the noise.

"Madame Foster!" the four of them cried out. (Well, Coco merely said, "Coco!" That was the only word she knew how to say.)

Madame Foster looked at Mac and the friends in surprise. "What? Oh, my, was I talking out loud?"

"Very loud!" said Eduardo.

"Sorry," apologized Madame Foster. "But that Jerkins had the gumption to bribe my girls away from me with handmade doilies!"

Nobody had any idea what Madame Foster was so upset about. Nobody but Mac, that is.

Being a smart kid, Mac had already figured out what Madame Foster really meant.

"Hold on, Madame Foster, let me see if I got this," he said. "This Jerkins lady has stolen your bowling team before the final game of the tournament by giving them doilies?"

"What, am I speakin' French here?" said Madame Foster, who thought that everything she'd said was very clear. "But now I'm done. That's it. That's all. Good night, nurse!"

But Mac didn't think that Madame Foster had to be out of the bowling tournament. "What about us?" Mac asked eagerly. "Me,

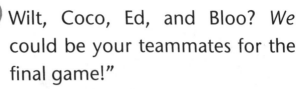

Wilt, Coco, Ed, and Bloo? *We* could be your teammates for the final game!"

Wilt, Coco, and Eduardo nodded in agreement.

"Really? You'd do that?" asked Madame Foster, with hope in her eyes.

"Glad to do it. Right, Bloo?" asked Mac, turning to his best friend.

But Bloo had been so busy with his Chinese finger puzzle, he had missed the entire conversation. "Wha?" he said, looking up.

"We'll be Madame Foster's new bowling team," said Mac, filling Bloo in.

"Not me," said Bloo with a grimace.

"Why not?" asked Mac.

"Bowling stinks," Bloo stated.

"Does not!" cried Madame Foster.

"Does, too. It's weak," added Bloo.

"This from the whiz kid," said Mac scornfully, pointing at Bloo's Chinese finger puzzle.

"Hey! *This* is tough!" said Bloo. "But bowling? Barely a sport. Like cavepeople throwing rocks at sticks."

"Fine, you're out!" Madame Foster shot back.

"But —" interjected Mac.

"Nope," said Madame Foster. "Actually, I only need four of ya. Ha! C'mon, time's a-wastin'! Let's go!"

Madame Foster picked up her ball and headed for the door. Wilt, Coco, and Eduardo followed. Mac started to head out, then turned back to Bloo.

"C'mon, Bloo," said Mac.

"Why am I going?" asked Bloo.

"What else have you got to do?" Mac asked.

"I got this," said Bloo, holding up his Chinese finger puzzle. His hands were still caught inside.

"Talk about weak," scoffed Mac.

FOSTER'S FIGHTERS

2

At the bowling alley, a group of old ladies wore matching pink bowling shirts that said FLO'S DOILY GOILS on the back. All the ladies were admiring the handmade doilies they had just been given. All except for a tall old lady with even taller hair. This was Flo Jerkins, and she was smiling proudly at having stolen her new team from Madame Foster.

"I did it! I won!" said Flo with a grin.

"I hated to do it, but the handiwork on this doily is simply remarkable," said Winnie, an old lady sitting on a scooter. She held her doily fondly.

"And they're so versatile," added Myrtle, who wore her doily on her head.

"Mmmm-hmmmm!" agreed Edie, who had her doily sitting under a plate of cookies.

"CAN'T WAIT TO PUT THIS BABY IN MY POWDER ROOM!" shouted Shirley, waving her doily in the air. (Shirley was having trouble with her hearing aid.)

But just as Flo and the Doily Goils were celebrating, something unexpected happened. *BANG!* The bowling alley doors flew open. The dark alley filled with sunlight. Flo and the Doily Goils gasped and shrank back as Madame Foster, Mac, Wilt, Coco, and Eduardo strutted into the bowling alley. They were wearing matching bowling shirts and looking fine.

Madame Foster had a new team: Foster's Fighters!

"Ha-ha! Did it! Showed ya! Take that!" said Madame Foster.

Flo bent down so she was nose to nose with Madame Foster. "What's this, Foster?" she demanded.

"My new team, Jerkins!" said Madame Foster proudly.

"Oh, yeah? Well, if you and this ragtag team are coming to the finals, you all better BRING IT!" hollered Flo.

"Oh, it's already BRUNG!" shouted Madame Foster, who was not afraid of Flo. "Come on, team, let's shoe up!" And with that, she led her players off to get their bowling shoes.

Meanwhile, Bloo was straggling behind, struggling with his Chinese finger puzzle. Then he saw something out of the corner of his eye. It was a claw machine called the Grabby Grab. Bloo was so amazed by the sight, he dropped his Chinese finger puzzle and rushed to the Grabby Grab. His eyes were drawn to one prize in particular: a paddleball!

"Ohhhhhhhhhhhh!" said Bloo longingly. He saw Mac heading toward the shoe counter and ran after him. "Quarter! Gimme a quarter!" Bloo cried.

"What?" asked Mac.

"Quarter, quarter, quarter!" Bloo begged.

"All right, man, chill out," said Mac as he dug in his pocket and pulled out a quarter. He handed it to Bloo, who ran off in a flash.

"You're welcome," Mac called after him. He was used to his Imaginary Friend's selfish antics.

Mac joined the gang at the shoe counter. Behind the counter was a case filled with huge, shiny bowling trophies. There were also pictures of a man with an Imaginary Friend who looked like a bowling pin. The man and the Imaginary Friend were dressed in matching bowling shirts, holding up the trophies they had won.

"Cool!" said Mac.

"Shoe, please," said a voice. Mac looked up to see that the man in the picture was standing behind the counter.

"Huh?" replied Mac, confused.

"To get your shoes, you've got to give a shoe," explained the man.

"Oh, yeah, right," said Mac. He took off his shoe and put it on the counter. The man handed him a pair of bowling shoes. Then it was Coco's turn.

"Shoe, please," said the man.

"Coco," replied Coco.

"Shoe, please," repeated the man.

"Coco," repeated Coco.

"Shoe . . ." the man began again. But Mac decided to jump in and stop this craziness.

"Yeah, she doesn't wear shoes," he explained.

The man peered over the counter at Coco's big, shoeless feet. "No shoe, no shoes," he said.

"Yeah, but . . ." said Mac.

"No shoe, no shoes," repeated the man.

Just then, Coco got a goofy look on her face. She laid a plastic egg, opened it, and pulled out a shiny new pair of bowling shoes. She put them on the counter for the man. He took them and gave her a pair of beat-up, stinky, old bowling shoes. Coco put them on with a smile and walked off to bowl.

As Coco headed toward the bowling lanes, she passed by Bloo, who was not doing well at the Grabby Grab.

"C'mon, c'mon, c'mon!" he begged as he tried to grab the paddleball with the claw. But he missed every time. Suddenly, the claw froze. Bloo's turn was over.

Bloo raced over to Mac. "Quarter, quarter, quarter!"

"I gave you a quarter," said Mac.

"Another quarter!" Bloo said insistently.

Mac sighed. He dug around in his pocket for a quarter.

"Here, take them," said Mac, handing Bloo a bunch of quarters.

"Yes!" cried Bloo, grabbing them away and running off again.

"You're welcome!" Mac called out again, knowing that he would never get a thank-you from Bloo.

GRAND MASTER MAC

3

Out on the lanes, Madame Foster was ready to get her new bowling team going.

"Wilt!" she called out. "Let's go!"

Wilt stepped up with his ball and started spinning it around. He passed it from hand to hand and rolled it over his shoulders. He even spun it on one finger. Flo and the Doily Goils' jaws dropped in amazement.

"This guy looks good," said Winnie, looking nervous.

But then Wilt tossed the ball in the air like

he was shooting a basketball. Everyone's eyes were wide as they watched it go up. *BANG!* It crashed down, making a huge dent in the lane.

"Or not," said Winnie, cringing from the thud.

Madame Foster came up close to Wilt. "Now, Wilt, honey, I appreciate the spit and polish, but THIS IS NOT BASKETBALL!" she hollered at him.

"Sorry," said Wilt apologetically. He hated to make anyone upset. Wilt wound up again and stretched his long arm down the lane with the ball still in his hand. Wilt's arm stretched so far, it nearly reached the pins. Then he let go of the ball. It rolled a little and knocked down all but one pin.

The Doily Goils couldn't believe it. But Flo was not impressed. "Pah! Beginner's luck," she commented.

"Yeah, but my beginner's a winner!" retorted Madame Foster. "See, Mac, we didn't need that little Bloo rain cloud anyhow!"

And speaking of Bloo, the Grabby Grab was raining on his parade. He kept trying for the paddleball — and missing. Finally, the claw froze again. Bloo's turn was finished. He pulled another quarter out.

"Bring me the magic, O shiny eagle!" he whispered as he slid another quarter into the machine. Bloo's eyes filled with joy as the claw began to move again.

Meanwhile, Eduardo's eyes filled with fear as he heard the loud crashing of bowling balls.

"Eduardo, stop being such a wimp!" exclaimed Madame Foster.

"Nooooooo! Too noisy! Too scary!" he cried, not wanting to pick up the ball.

"I'm sorry, Eddie," Madame Foster said softly. "I just meant, STOP BEING SUCH A WIMP!" she shouted at Eduardo, who shook in fear.

Wilt stepped up to help out. "It's okay, Eduardo," Wilt said in a soothing tone. "Don't make it bang. Just let it down easy."

Eduardo walked up to the lane and put his ball on the floor. He put it on the ground and gave it a push. The ball rolled down the lane slowly. Very, very slowly.

"It's a creeper!" Flo said to her teammates as they all watched the ball creep down the lane.

Eduardo grew more and more nervous as the ball got closer to the pins. He chewed on his nails, scared that the ball was going to make a big, scary noise. When the ball finally hit the pins, it knocked them all down in slow motion. They barely made a peep.

"Ah! That not so bad," Eduardo said, relieved.

"NOT SO BAD!" shouted Madame Foster. She was excited that Eduardo had gotten a strike. But she only scared Eduardo all the more.

Madame Foster turned to Coco next. "COCO, YOU'RE UP!" she hollered.

Coco walked up to the lane in her bowling shoes. She slipped one foot out of a shoe, grabbed the ball with her foot, and hurled it. The only problem was, she threw the ball behind her! Everyone ducked as the ball flew overhead. The ball shot straight back and lodged itself in the wall right above the Grabby Grab. But Bloo was so busy trying to get the paddleball, he didn't even notice. The claw had just frozen once again, much to Bloo's annoyance.

Bloo pulled out another quarter and rubbed it in his hands. "C'mon, Georgie!" he said to the quarter, sliding it into the machine.

Back at the lanes, Madame Foster grabbed Coco and turned her around. Now Coco's back was toward the pins. Madame Foster set up the ball behind Coco's foot. Coco grabbed the ball, threw it back, and knocked over eight pins with a BANG!

"Now we're cookin' with fire!" crowed Madame Foster. "All right, let's see what you got, Grand Master Mac!" Madame Foster turned toward Flo and the Doily Goils. "This kid is the mastermind behind this whole team!"

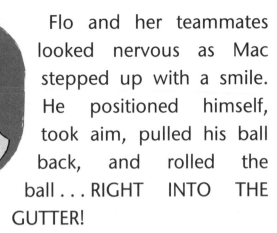

Flo and her teammates looked nervous as Mac stepped up with a smile. He positioned himself, took aim, pulled his ball back, and rolled the ball . . . RIGHT INTO THE GUTTER!

"WHAT!" shouted a stunned Madame Foster.

"That's your mastermind? Brilliant!" said Flo. She and the Doily Goils burst out laughing.

"Hey! That was my first time! Watch this!" responded Mac.

Mac grabbed his ball, aimed, and threw. At first, the ball headed down the center of the lane. It looked like Mac was actually going to get a strike. But then, right before the ball hit the pins, it turned to the left and knocked one pin down.

"What!" cried Madame Foster.

"Woo-hoo!" yelled Mac. He twirled around on his tiptoes, proud of what he'd done.

Madame Foster waited till the end of his happy dance. Then she put her arm around Mac. "Why, that's very good, Mac," she said sweetly. "Only one problem. YOU STINK!" she shouted. Then she turned back to the rest of her team. "The rest of you better pony up to the plate to make up for this rotten apple!"

THE DOILY GOILS VS. FOSTER'S FIGHTERS

4

At the Grabby Grab, Bloo was pleading with the machine. "Please! I've given you what you want. Now help me get what I want. You wouldn't miss that old paddleball anyhow. And you would know it was going to a good home. To someone who would shelter it, love it, paddle it. So, c'mon, let's work together

here so that everyone can be happy!"

Bloo put in another quarter. He moved the claw down to the paddleball. It looked

like it was going to grab it when . . . it missed!
"This game is a dork!" Bloo shouted angrily.

Back with the bowlers, Madame Foster threw her ball down the lane. She knocked down eight pins. But the two that were left were spread far apart. Madame Foster's jaw dropped.

Flo was smiling. "The 7–10 Split. Nice." It was going to be almost impossible for Madame Foster to knock both pins down.

But Madame Foster had a determined look in her eye as she threw her ball. It rolled down the lane and knocked one pin down. As that pin fell, it slid over and hit the last pin.

"Woo-hoo!" Madame Foster shouted gleefully. "Pickin' up the bedposts!"

On Flo's next throw, she threw a perfect strike, knocking down all the pins.

"I'm slammin' it tonight!" she shouted as her teammates cheered.

Next, Wilt wound up his arm so it was going really fast. He threw the ball down the lane for a strike. He did a celebratory moonwalk, twirled, and landed in a split.

"Gettin' nervous there, Jerkins? Shakin' in your orthopedic boots?" said Madame Foster to her old rival. But before Flo could answer, Mac stepped up to bowl. And once again, he knocked down just one pin.

"Yeah, not so much," answered Flo as she watched Mac's terrible bowling.

It was Doily Goil Myrtle's turn to bowl. Myrtle approached the lane slowly, using her walker to help her move the ball up to the lane. Wilt, Coco, Eduardo, and Mac smirked, figuring Myrtle wouldn't be able to hit any-thing. But she gave the ball a little kick with her walker, and it rolled slowly but surely down the lane, knocking down all the pins. The friends heaved a sigh of annoyance.

Coco walked up to her lane, turned around, and laid a plastic egg. The egg rolled a few feet, popped open, and a bowling ball came out. It zoomed down the lane. Coco got a strike!

Winnie came up in her scooter with her bowling ball in the front basket. She released the ball from the basket, and it slammed the pins down for another strike. Winnie spun around and around in her scooter in celebration. Flo and the Doily Goils were doing great!

Eduardo went up for his next throw. But as he picked up the ball, Flo surprised him. "Boo!" she yelled, scaring Eduardo.

"Aaaah!" he screamed, flinging the ball into the air. Flo and the Doily Goils laughed at this big guy being so afraid. But the joke was on

them as Eduardo's ball landed smack in the middle of the lane and knocked down all of his pins.

"Ha-ha-ha! You big meanies!" laughed Eduardo as Flo stormed off.

Edie was up next. She picked up a spare by knocking down the last four pins on her second throw.

Things were not looking good for Foster's Fighters. Especially when Mac threw a gutter ball on his next turn. Flo and the Doily Goils couldn't stop laughing.

"Hey, Foster! Maybe you oughta change your name from Foster's Fighters to Foster's Flatulence. Because you stink!" said Flo.

That really got Madame Foster steamed. She marched over to Mac, who was getting ready to take his next turn.

"Mac?" she said in a tender voice. "I got some advice for you. You see this ball? I need you to take it and HIT SOME BLOOMIN' PINS!"

"Huh," Mac sighed. He got up to bowl. He took a deep breath and concentrated on the pins. That's when Bloo came running up.

"Quarter," said Bloo.

"Not now," said Mac.

"Quarter!" demanded Bloo.

"Hold on," said Mac, trying to concentrate.

"QUARTER!" Bloo insisted.

"Just a minute!" said Mac. He was determined to hit at least two pins this time. He didn't want to let the team down.

"Quarter, quarter, quarter, quarter!" cried Bloo, bouncing up and down anxiously.

"BLOO! I'm tryin' to bowl here!" shouted Mac.

But Bloo still thought bowling was a dumb game. "So weak!" he exclaimed, grabbing the ball from Mac. Without even looking, he tossed it down the lane.

"Bloo, you don't understand," Mac started to explain. "I really have to get a . . ."

CRASH! Bloo's ball flew down the lane and knocked all the pins down.

"STRIKE?" said Mac, stunned.

BOWLING PAUL

Mac couldn't believe it. Bloo had gotten a strike without even trying!

"Quarter!" Bloo repeated. But before Mac could respond, Madame Foster came running up.

"Bloo, did you do that?" she said eagerly.

"Yeah, what of it?" said Bloo carelessly.

Madame Foster pointed up at the computer screen above the lane. It had a big *X* on it.

"That's what of it!" cried Madame Foster. She yanked Mac's bowling shirt off and handed it to Bloo. "Bloo, try this on for size."

"What? But . . ." said a stunned Mac.

"No buts. You're bad. He's good. He's in. You're out!" said Madame Foster.

"But, but, but . . . I wanna be part of the team!" cried Mac.

"You wanna be part of the team, go polish the balls, go shine the shoes, go get some nachos. Just DON'T BOWL!" Madame Foster shouted.

Mac slumped off, defeated.

Madame Foster turned to Bloo. "Bloo, with you on our team, we may be able to bring this cow back in from the pasture."

"Yeah, yeah," said Bloo, hardly listening. "You got a quarter?"

"Here you go, boy," said Madame Foster, handing him a pile of quarters. "Quarters galore. Just remember, when I call your name, you work your magic."

"Anything you say, lady. Anything you say," Bloo said, staring at all the wonderful quarters. He was sure to get his paddleball now!

Mac was muttering angrily to himself as he walked away. "Stupid bowling with its stupid shoes and its stupid balls . . ." But then his eyes fell on something amazing. Or some*one* amazing. It was the Imaginary Bowling Friend he had seen in the pictures in the trophy case! He was shaped like a bowling pin with a bowling-pin head. He wore bowling shoes, a bowling shirt, bowling gloves, and sunglasses. This dude was cool!

Mac took a deep breath and approached the Bowling Friend,

who was busy polishing his bowling ball. "Excuse me?"

"Yes?" said the Bowling Friend in a smooth, soothing tone.

Mac gestured toward the pictures in the trophy case. "You're the friend from the pictures?" asked Mac. He was totally in awe of the Bowling Friend.

"Yes, that is me. Bowling Paul," he answered, bowing. "How can I help you, son?"

Mac was so excited, he could hardly speak. He was talking to the guru of bowling. Clearly, with all those trophies, this guy was the best bowler ever. Mac tried to explain how much he needed Bowling Paul's help.

"See, I really want to learn how to bowl really, really well. And I mean, you . . . in the pictures . . . all those trophies. Do . . . do you think you could . . . teach me?" asked Mac.

"Why, yes," said the serene Bowling Paul. "I can teach you the way of the ball. The question is, are you ready?"

"I am so ready," said Mac, eager to get started.

"Then let us begin," said Bowling Paul. "Take your ball. . . ."

"I don't have a ball," Mac interrupted.

"Then, my child, you do not have a soul," said Bowling Paul.

"Yeah, but . . . I can get a ball," said Mac. He didn't see what the big deal was.

"You think souls are so easy to come by?" asked Bowling Paul doubtfully.

"Well, uh, they have a bunch of balls over there on the rack," said Mac, pointing at the many balls he had to choose from. He zipped off, grabbed a ball, and zipped back again.

"Okay!" said Mac. He held up his ball, ready to start bowling.

"Good, good. Now, first: You are the ball," Bowling Paul instructed.

"I am the ball," repeated Mac.

"The ball is you," Bowling Paul continued.

"The ball is me," repeated Mac.

"Without the ball, you are nothing," finished Bowling Paul.

"Got it," said Mac, who was ready to move on to some bowling.

Bowling Paul pointed down at the pins at the end of the lane. "Now, you see those pins?" he asked.

"Yeah," said Mac, looking down the lane.

"You are those pins," said Bowling Paul.

"But I thought I was the ball," said Mac, confused.

"You are also the pins," Bowling Paul instructed.

"Oh. Okay," said Mac. He was still a little confused as to how he could be the ball *and* the pins. But he figured Bowling Paul must know what he was talking about.

"The pins are you," Bowling Paul added.

"And without the pins I am nothing?" said Mac. He had a good idea where Bowling Paul's speech was going.

"You are a wise boy," said Bowling Paul, impressed.

"Yeah, I'm pretty quick on the uptake. Now, what about bowling?" asked Mac, who was really getting anxious to move on to the actual bowling part of the bowling lesson.

"No bowling," said Bowling Paul.

"No bowling?" repeated Mac, stunned.

"You are not ready for such a step," said Bowling Paul.

"I think I am," said Mac.

"No. When the time is right, all elements of the game will align and you will bowl like none have bowled before."

Mac was happy to hear this. "That's cool! 'Cause all I want to do is bowl as well as Bloo!"

THE WAY OF
THE BALL

Speaking of Bloo, Madame Foster was call-
ing for the newest and best player on her
team. "BLOO!" she cried, trying to grab his
attention away from the Grabby Grab.

Bloo came running over, and Madame Foster handed him a ball. Without even looking,
he threw the ball down the lane and knocked
all the pins down.

"Strike one!" shouted Madame Foster.

Back on the other side of the alley, Mac was
standing blindfolded, swinging the bowling
ball back and forth.

"Feel the weight of the ball," instructed

Bowling Paul. "Feel the power of your arms. You don't need your eyes. They will deceive you, fool you, be your downfall. Trust in your ball. Trust in your soul. If I could rename this game it would be *souling*, not bowling. And I would be Souling Paul. And we would be at the souling alley, throwing our souls down the lane to the pins of life, seeing which way they fell."

A tear fell from behind Mac's blindfold. "That's beautiful," said Mac.

"I know," said Bowling Paul.

But while Mac and Bowling Paul were having a meaningful moment, Madame Foster wanted only one thing. "BLOO!" she cried.

Bloo came running up again. He picked up his ball, threw it, and slammed the pins down once again.

"Strike two!" Madame Foster shrieked with glee.

Bowling Paul held up a bowling pin in front of Mac's face. "This is the enemy," he told Mac.

"But I thought this was me," said Mac. He was confused again.

"It is you," confirmed Bowling Paul. "This is your dark side. And you must control the dark side."

"With my mind?" asked Mac.

"With your ball," said Bowling Paul.

"Ah!" said Mac. He was starting to understand the way of the ball.

But Madame Foster had no need for the way of the ball. All she needed was . . .

"BLOO!"

Bloo ran in, grabbed the ball, tossed it down the lane, and knocked over all the pins.

"Strike three!" Madame Foster shouted.

Bowling Paul looked down the lane. "You see, life is like a narrow road," said Bowling Paul. He pointed to the right gutter of the lane. "We can walk on the right." He pointed to the left gutter. "We can walk on the left." Then he pointed down the center of the lane. "Or we can walk down the middle."

"Isn't walking down the middle of a road dangerous?" interrupted Mac.

"In walking, yes. But in *bowling*," said Bowling Paul, "the middle of the road leads us to victory."

"Sweet, sweet victory!" said Mac, liking the sound of it.

Madame Foster was beginning to taste a little victory of her own as she called for her star player once more. "BLOOOOOOO!"

Once again, Bloo dashed up, picked up his ball, and tossed it. It rolled down the lane, going this way and that. "Oh, no!" shouted Madame Foster. But she didn't need to worry.

Bloo's ball sent all the pins flying.

"Yes! Woo-hoo!" Madame Foster cried. She smirked at Flo. "That ring-a-ding-dinger has just hopped, skipped, and jumped us into the lead, Jerkins!"

Flo turned away, seething mad. "That festering Foster has been a fly in my face cream for too long. Something's gotta be done. Even if I have to beg, borrow, or . . ." Suddenly, Flo had an idea. She looked over at the little figure at the Grabby Grab. "Or BLOO!" she finished, grinning evilly.

DOILY BLOO

 **7**

Bowling Paul looked at Mac, proud of what he saw. "You are ready, my son," he told him. "I've taught you all that can be taught and you have learned all that can be learned. Now, pick up your soul and bowl in peace."

Mac picked up his ball, enlightened by what Bowling Paul had taught him. But a shout of horror soon broke that peace.

"NOOOOOOOOOOO!" shrieked Bloo. He was plastered against the Grabby Grab with a pained look on his face. Inside the Grabby Grab, the paddleball was GONE! "How could it be? How could all I've worked for be gone, gone, gone!"

But it wasn't gone. Suddenly Bloo saw something out of the corner of his eye. He turned toward it in awe. It was THE PADDLEBALL!

Meanwhile, Madame Foster was busy looking up at the computer scorecard, cackling with glee. "Ha-ha-ha-ha-ha! Did you ever see anything more perfect than this?! Let's put the final nail in this bad boy! Bloo! Bloo-hoo! Bloo?"

"Yoo-hoo!" called Flo, trying to get Madame Foster's attention.

Madame Foster turned to see her worst nightmare: Bloo in a Doily Goils bowling shirt. Madame Foster shook her head in disbelief. "Bloo, what are you . . ." she began, letting her words trail off as she gazed at Bloo.

He hadn't heard a word. "Paddleball, paddleball," he repeated over and over as he stared up at the paddleball. Flo was holding it in front of him, hypnotizing him by swinging its little red ball back and forth.

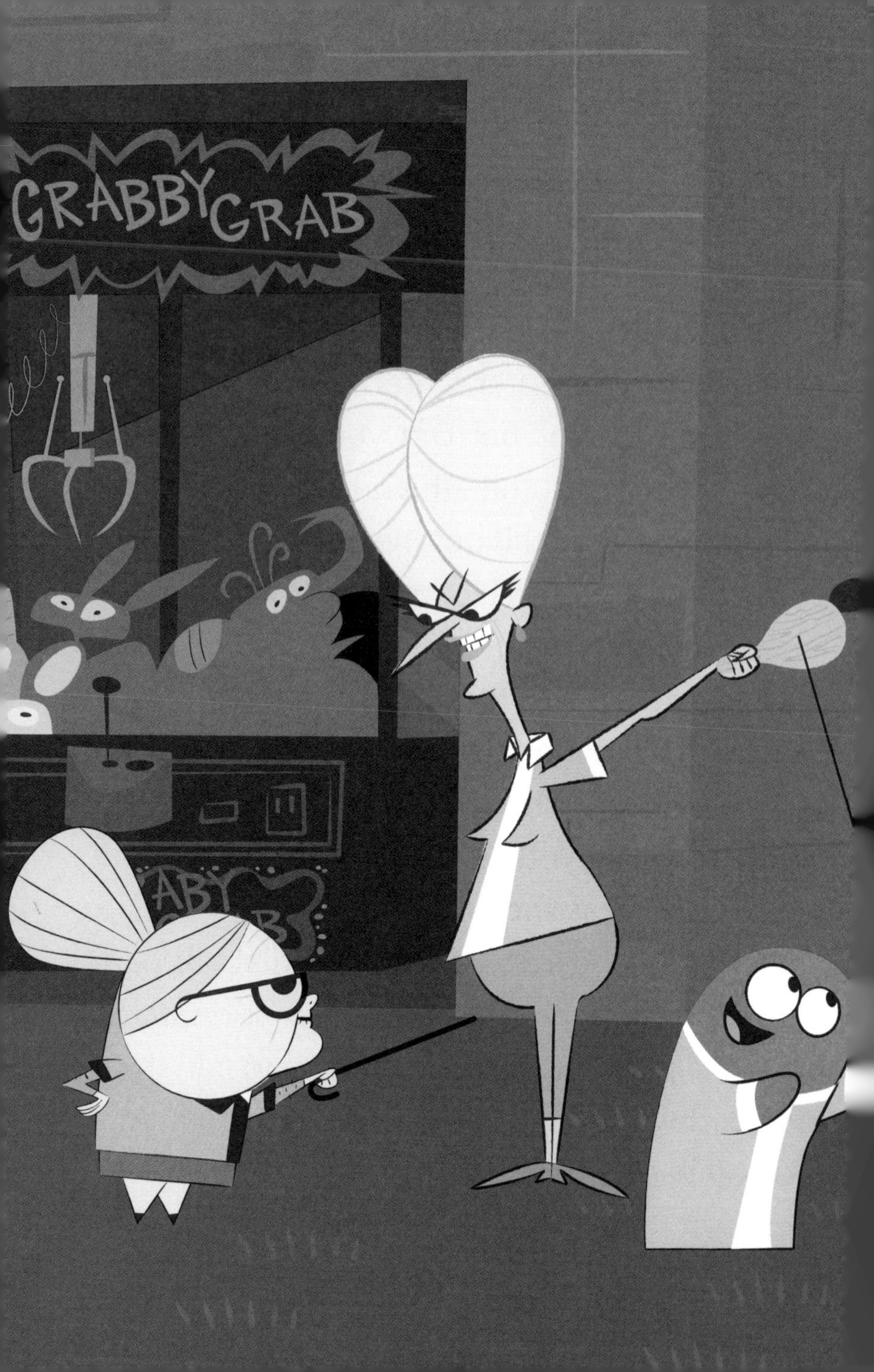
GRABBY GRAB

Madame Foster stormed up to Flo. "Jerkins, you ringworm! Give him back!"

"Are you bananas, Foster?" asked Flo. "There's one more frame and this bonnie Bloo is going to rocket us right to the top!"

"But you've got enough players!" Madame Foster objected.

"Well, there's been a bit of a tragedy," said Flo, pretending to be sad. "Winnie's run out of juice." She pointed at her old teammate.

"C'mon, c'mon!" cried Winnie, trying to start her scooter. Shirley and Edie snickered at the sight. They were trying to hide the battery from Winnie's scooter behind their backs.

Madame Foster was appalled. "You took down one of your own?!"

"Now, don't act all high and mighty. You threw that boy away like an old pair of support hose. C'mon, Bloo, let's finish this game," said Flo. And she led Bloo off, dangling the paddle-ball just out of his reach.

Madame Foster stood stunned. She realized that Flo was right. And she was ashamed.

The rest of her team looked at her, not knowing what to do. Finally, Wilt spoke up. "I hate to have to say it, Madame Foster, but maybe we have to throw in the towel."

"Oh, no, you don't!" said a voice. Foster's Fighters looked over and gasped in shock. It was Mac, all decked out Bowling Paul style. "'Cause you've got me!" he declared proudly.

Madame Foster, Wilt, Coco, and Eduardo couldn't help but crack up at this.

"But don't you remember, dear?" Madame Foster said gently. "You stink."

"But I've been taking lessons," said Mac hopefully.

"Bowling lessons?" asked Madame Foster doubtfully.

Mac was not amused. "Yes, bowling les-sons."

"So, you're telling me that you can assure our victory by rolling that ball, getting a strike, and winning the game?" Madame Foster asked doubtfully.

"What, am I speaking French here?" said Mac. He was confident of his abilities. "Watch and be stupefied!"

THE FINAL
BOWL-DOWN

8

Over with the Doily Goils, Flo rubbed Bloo's shoulders, prepping him for the final frame. "It's almost yours, Bloo. You win this for me, and that paddleball is goin' home with you."

"Ooooooooh!" said Bloo, delirious at the thought. He stepped up to his lane, right beside Mac.

Mac was mentally preparing himself to bowl, just as Bowling Paul taught him. "I am the ball. I am the pins. The pins are my enemy. I am my enemy. I must roll my soul down the center of the lane and destroy my enemy, thus destroy-

ing myself, but in destroying myself, find peace."

Bloo was preparing himself mentally as well. "Paddleball. Paddleball. Paddleball."

Mac closed his eyes, trusting in the way of the ball.

Bloo looked down the lane, determined to succeed and get his paddleball.

Together, Mac and Bloo pulled back their bowling balls. Bloo released his, and it zoomed right down the center of the lane toward the pins.

"Yes!" cried Flo, knowing that her team was sure to be victorious.

Then, feeling fully prepared, Mac released his ball as well. But instead of zooming down the lane like Bloo's, Mac's ball went flying across *all* the lanes.

Madame Foster was shocked. "No!"

Mac opened his eyes just as his ball hit a wall. "What? But I took lessons!" he cried, ducking as the ball came whizzing back at him.

"Lessons on stinkin' worse?" said Madame Foster as she dodged the ball flying overhead.

"No!" cried Mac.

"Lessons from him!" said Mac, pointing at Bowling Paul.

"Him?" said another voice. Everyone looked to see that it was the man who'd given them all bowling shoes earlier. It was the same man who was in all the pictures with Bowling Paul and the trophies. In fact, he was also the owner

of the bowling alley. He ducked as Mac's bowling ball came flying by. "He can't bowl for beans!"

"What?" said Mac in shock. "Yes, he can! Just look at him!" He pointed at Bowling Paul, who was polishing his bowling ball. "The pictures . . . the trophies!" protested Mac as his ball went crashing into the trophy case.

"All mine," said the owner of the bowling alley. "Paul's my Imaginary Friend and he's in those pictures with me. But *I'm* the one who won all those trophies."

"But he's Bowling Paul!" said a desperate Mac. "You created him. Shouldn't that mean he can bowl?"

Mac's ball came sailing by again. "He is," the man said, ducking. "I did." He ducked again. "It should." He ducked once more. "But it don't," he said, ducking a final time.

Mac looked at Bowling Paul, who was crouching down as the ball zipped by. "Sorry, kid," he said, shrugging.

Mac's ball smashed into the Grabby Grab, and the little girl went running up to snatch some free toys. Then Mac's ball went bouncing across the lanes and hit Bloo's ball, knocking it out of Bloo's lane. Then Mac's ball jumped back into his own lane and knocked down all his pins. *STRIKE!*

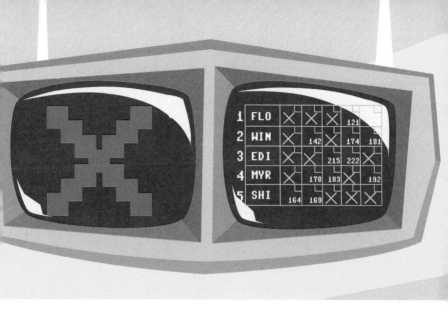

1	FLO	X	X	X	121	
2	WIN	X	142	X	174	181
3	EDI	X	X	215	222	X
4	MYR	X	178	183	X	192
5	SHI	164	169	X	X	X

"What?" cried Mac.

"What?" screeched Madame Foster.

"What?" shrieked Flo.

"Paddleball?" whimpered Bloo.

The computer scorecard flashed a huge *X* over their heads. It was indeed a strike!

Madame Foster threw her arms up in victory. "Yes!"

Flo fell to her knees. "Nooooooo!"

Wilt, Coco, and Eduardo cheered at Mac's success.

Madame Foster hugged Mac. "Jumpin' bird dogs, Mac, those lousy bowling lessons won us the game!"

"What? Really?" said Mac, unable to believe it.

"Really!" confirmed Madame Foster.

"Wow! So, where's the trophy?" asked Mac.

Madame Foster looked at him, stunned. "Trophy! We didn't win any trophy. They did!" she said, gesturing over to a totally different team that was celebrating their victory.

Mac and the gang were stunned. "What? Qué? Coco?" they all cried together.

"We weren't competing for first place. That's for the good teams. We were competing for fifth!" said Madame Foster.

"Fifth!" Mac exclaimed.

"Yep," confirmed Flo, stepping up. "And I nearly gotcha this time, Foster."

"Not on your tintype, Jerkins!" said Madame

Foster. "I had it in my hip pocket the whole time!"

"Yeah, right!" said Flo with a sneer. "So, we on next Sunday for tea?"

"Tea?" asked Mac in amazement.

"And crumpets!" added Madame Foster.

"Crumpets! But I thought Jerkins was your archrival!" said Mac, confused.

"Doesn't mean we can't act civilized now and again!" said Madame Foster with a smile.

Flo and the Doily Goils turned to leave when a desperate Bloo approached Flo. "Paddleball? Paddleball?" he begged.

Flo pulled out the paddleball. "You mean this?" she taunted him, holding it out of his reach.

"Yes, yes!" cried Bloo, grabbing at it.

"After that slipshod performance? Forget it!" said Flo. She threw the paddleball to the floor and walked off.

Bloo's eyes went wide with horror as the paddleball fell toward the floor. "Nooooo!" He lunged for it, grabbing it just in time. "Phew!"

Madame Foster and the gang just shook their heads at this pitiful display. But Bloo wasn't about to let that stop him. He stood up and tried to paddle. Trouble was, he stank.

"Ow! C'mon! Ow! Man! Ouch! Hey!" he

cried as he attempted to hit the ball. But he kept whacking himself in the face and tangling the elastic around his body.

Mac watched his friend and shook his head. "Bloo, it's a paddleball."

"Yeah. And it's hard!" cried Bloo, pummeling himself with the toy. "Gimme that," said Mac, grabbing the toy from Bloo.

"You're so cool, lemme see you do it," challenged Bloo.

Mac gave Bloo a sly look and began to paddle away. He paddled around his body, under his leg, and even changed hands. He was brilliant.

Bloo's jaw dropped in shock. "Wha-hunh?"

"Now who's weak?" said Mac, grinning. He walked off, paddling as he went.

Then Bloo heard a voice

behind him. "I can help you, my son."

Bloo slowly turned to see an Imaginary Friend shaped like a huge paddleball. He was  paddling a paddleball skillfully.

"I am Paddle Paul," said the guru of paddleball.

Bloo gazed at him in awe. He knew he had found the true paddleball master.